Samuel Taylor Coleridge, Robert Southey

The Fall of Robespierre

Samuel Taylor Coleridge, Robert Southey

The Fall of Robespierre

ISBN/EAN: 9783337376833

Printed in Europe, USA, Canada, Australia, Japan

Cover: Foto ©Andreas Hilbeck / pixelio.de

More available books at **www.hansebooks.com**

THE

FALL

OF

ROBESPIERRE.

AN

HISTORIC DRAMA.

BY S. T. COLERIDGE,

OF JESUS COLLEGE, CAMBRIDGE.

𝕮𝖆𝖒𝖇𝖗𝖎𝖉𝖌𝖊 :

PRINTED BY BENJAMIN FLOWER,

FOR W. H. LUNN, AND J. AND J. MERRILL ; AND SOLD
BY J. MARCH, NORWICH.

1794.

TO

H. MARTIN, Esq.

OF

JESUS COLLEGE,

CAMBRIDGE.

DEAR SIR,

ACCEPT, as a fmall teftimony of my grateful attachment, the following Dramatic Poem, in which I have endeavoured to detail, in an interefting form, the fall of a man, whofe great bad actions have caft a difaftrous luftre on his name. In the execution of the work, as intricacy of plot could not have been attempted without a grofs violation of recent facts, it has been my fole aim to imitate the empaffioned and highly figurative language of the French Orators, and to develope the characters of the chief actors on a vaft ftage of horrors.

Yours fraternally,
S. T. COLERIDGE.

Jefus College,
September 22, 1794.

THE
FALL OF ROBESPIERRE.

ACT I.

SCENE, The Thuilleries.

BARRERE.

THE tempeſt gathers—be it mine to ſeek
A friendly ſhelter, ere it burſts upon him.
But where? and how? I fear the Tyrant's *ſoul*—
Sudden in action, fertile in reſource,
And riſing awful 'mid impending ruins;
In ſplendor gloomy, as the midnight meteor,
That fearleſs thwarts the elemental war.
When laſt in ſecret conference we met,
He ſcowl'd upon me with ſuſpicious rage,
Making his eye the inmate of my boſom.
I know he ſcorns me—and I feel, I hate him—
Yet there is in him that which makes me tremble!

                        (Exit.)

Enter TALLIEN *and* LEGENDRE.

TALLIEN.

It was Barrere, Legendre! didſt thou mark him?
Abrupt he turn'd, yet linger'd as he went,
And towards us caſt a look of doubtful meaning.

LEGENDRE.

I mark'd him well. I met his eye's laſt glance;
It menac'd not ſo proudly as of yore.
Methought he would have ſpoke—but that he dar'd not—
Such agitation darken'd on his brow.

B

TALLIEN.

'Twas all-diftrufting guilt that kept from burfting
Th' imprifon'd fecret ftruggling in the face:
E'en as the fudden breeze upftarting onwards
Hurries the thunder cloud, that pois'd awhile
Hung in mid air, red with its mutinous burthen.

LEGENDRE.

Perfidious Traitor!—ftill afraid to balk
In the full blaze of power, the ruftling ferpent
Lurks in the thicket of the Tyrant's greatnefs,
Ever prepar'd to fting who fhelters him.
Each thought, each action in himfelf converges;
And love and friendfhip on his coward heart
Shine like the powerlefs fun on polar ice:
To all attach'd, by turns deferting all,
Cunning and dark—a neceffary villain!

TALLIEN.

Yet much depends upon him—well you know
With plaufible harangue 'tis his to paint
Defeat like victory—and blind the mob
With truth-mix'd falfhood. They led on by him,
And wild of head to work their own deftruction,
Support with uproar what he plans in darknefs.

LEGENDRE.

O what a precious name is Liberty
To fcare or cheat the fimple into flaves!
Yes—we muft gain him over: by dark hints
We'll fhew enough to roufe his watchful fears,
Till the cold coward blaze a patriot.
O Danton! murder'd friend! affift my counfels—
Hover around me on fad memory's wings,
And pour thy daring vengeance in my heart:
Tallien! if but to-morrow's fateful fun
Beholds the Tyrant living—we are dead!

TALLIEN.

Yet his keen eye that flashes mighty meanings—

LEGENDRE.

Fear not—or rather fear th' alternative,
And seek for courage e'en in cowardice——
But see—hither he comes—let us away !
His brother with him, and the bloody Couthon,
And high of haughty spirit, young St. Just.

(*Exeunt.*)

Enter ROBESPIERRE, COUTHON, ST. JUST, *and*
ROBESPIERRE, *Junior.*

ROBESPIERRE.

What? did La Fayette fall before my power?
And did I conquer Roland's spotless virtues?
The fervent eloquence of Vergniaud's tongue?
And Brissot's thoughtful soul unbribed and bold?
Did zealot armies haste in vain to save them ?
What ! did th' assassin's dagger aim its point
Vain, as a *dream* of murder, at my bosom?
And shall I dread the soft luxurious Tallien ?
Th' Adonis Tallien? banquet-hunting Tallien?
Him, whose heart flutters at the dice-box? Him,
Who ever on the harlots' downy pillow
Resigns his head impure to feverish slumbers !

ST. JUST.

I cannot fear him—yet we must not scorn him.
Was it not Antony that conquer'd Brutus,
Th' Adonis, banquet-hunting Antony ?
The state is not yet purified : and though
The stream runs clear, yet at the bottom lies
The thick black sediment of all the factions—
It needs no magic hand to stir it up !

COUTHON.

O we did wrong to fpare them—fatal error !
Why lived Legendre, when that Danton died ?
And Collot d'Herbois dangerous in crimes?
I've fear'd him, fince his iron heart endured
To make of Lyons one vaft human fhambles,
Compar'd with which the fun-fcorcht wildernefs
Of Zara, were a fmiling paradife.

ST. JUST.

Rightly thou judgeft, Couthon ! He is one,
Who flies from filent folitary anguifh,
Seeking forgetful peace amid the jar
Of elements. The howl of maniac uproar
Lulls to fad fleep the memory of himfelf.
A calm is fatal to him—then he feels
The dire upboilings of the ftorm within him.
A tyger mad with inward wounds !——I dread
The fierce and reftlefs turbulence of guilt.

ROBESPIERRE.

Is not the commune ours ?　The ftern tribunal ?
Dumas? and Vivier? Fleuriot? and Louvet?
And Henriot? We'll denounce an hundred, nor
Shall they behold to-morrow's fun roll weftward.

ROBESPIERRE, Junior.

Nay—I am fick of blood ; my aching heart
Reviews the long, long train of hideous horrors
That ftill have gloom'd the rife of the republic.
I fhould have died before Toulon, when war
Became the patriot !

ROBESPIERRE.

　　　　　　　Moft unworthy wifh !
He, whofe heart fickens at the blood of traitors
Would be himfelf a traitor, were he not

A coward! 'Tis congenial fouls alone
Shed tears of forrow for each other's fate.
O thou art brave, my brother! and thine eye
Full firmly fhines amid the groaning battle—
Yet in thine heart the woman-form of pity
Afferts too large a fliare, an ill-timed gueft!
There is unfoundnefs in the ftate—To-morrow
Shall fee it cleans'd by wholefome maffacre!

ROBESPIERRE, Junior.

Beware! already do the fections murmur—
" O the great glorious patriot, Robefpierre—
" The *tyrant guardian* of the country's *freedom!*"

COUTHON.

Twere folly fure to work great deeds by halves!
Much I fufpect the darkfome fickle heart
Of cold Barrere!

ROBESPIERRE,
                    I fee the villain in him!

ROBESPIERRE, Junior.

If he—if all forfake thee—what remains?

ROBESPIERRE,

Myfelf! the fteel-ftrong Rectitude of foul
And Poverty fublime 'mid circling virtues!
The giant Victories, my counfels form'd,
Shall ftalk around me with fun-glittering plumes,
Bidding the darts of calumny fall pointlefs.
                    (*Exeunt cateri.* Manet Couthon.)

COUTHON *folus.*

So we deceive ourfelves! What goodly virtues
Bloom on the poifonous branches of ambition!
Still, Robefpierre! thou'l't guard thy country's freedom.

To defpotize in all the patriot's pomp.
While Confcience, 'mid the mob's applauding clamours,
Sleeps in thine ear, nor whifpers—blood-ftain'd tyrant!
Yet what is Confcience? Superftition's dream,
Making fuch deep impreffion on our fleep—
That long th' awaken'd breaft retains its horrors !
But he returns—and with him comes Barrere.

(Exit, Couthon.)

Enter Robespierre and Barrere.

ROBESPIERRE.

There is no danger but in cowardice.—
Barrere ! we *make* the danger, when we *fear* it.
We have fuch force without, as will fufpend
The cold and trembling treachery of thefe members.

BARRERE.

'Twill be a paufe of terror.—

ROBESPIERRE.

But to whom ?

Rather the fhort-lived flumber of the tempeft,
Gathering its ftrength anew. The daftard traitors !
Moles, that would undermine the rooted oak !
A paufe !—a *moment's* paufe ?—'Tis all *their life.*

BARRERE.

Yet much they talk—and plaufible their fpeech.
Couthon's decree has given fuch powers, that

ROBESPIERRE.

That what ?

BARRERE.

The freedom of debate—

ROBESPIERRE.
                        Tranſparent maſk !
They wiſh to clog the wheels of government,
Forcing the hand that guides the vaſt machine
To bribe them to their duty—*Engliſh* patriots !
Are not the congregated clouds of war
Black all around us? In our very vitals
Works not the king-bred poiſon of rebellion ?
Say, what ſhall counteract the ſelfiſh plottings
Of wretches, cold of heart, nor awed by fears
Of him, whoſe power directs th' eternal juſtice?
Terror? or ſecret-ſapping gold? The firſt
Heavy, but tranſient as the ills that cauſe it ;
And to the virtuous patriot rendered light
By the neceſſities that gave it birth :
The other fouls the fount of the republic,
Making it flow polluted to all ages :
Inoculates the ſtate with a ſlow venom,
That once imbibed, muſt be continued ever.
Myſelf incorruptible I ne'er could bribe them—
Therefore they hate me.

BARRERE.
                        Are the ſections friendly ?

ROBESPIERRE.
There are who wiſh my ruin—but I'll make them
Bluſh for the crime in blood !

BARRERE.
                        Nay—but I tell thee,
Thou art too fond of ſlaughter—and the right
(If right it be) workeſt by moſt foul means !

ROBESPIERRE.
Self-centering Fear! how well thou canſt ape *Mercy !*
Too fond of ſlaughter !—matchleſs hypocrite !

Thought Barrere fo, when Briſſot, Danton died?
Thought Barrere fo, when through the ſtreaming ſtreets
Of Paris red-eyed Maſſacre o'er wearied
Reel'd heavily, intoxicate with blood?
And when (O heavens!) in Lyons' death-red ſquare
Sick fancy groan'd o'er putrid hills of ſlain,
Didſt thou not fiercely laugh, and bleſs the day?
Why, thou haſt been the mouth-piece of all horrors,
And, like a blood-hound, crouch'd for murder! Now
Aloof thou ſtandeſt from the tottering pillar,
Or, like a frighted child behind its mother,
Hideſt thy pale face in the ſkirts of—*Mercy!*

BARRERE.
O prodigality of eloquent anger!
Why now I ſee thou'rt weak—thy caſe is deſperate!
The cool ferocious Robeſpierre turn'd ſcolder!

ROBESPIERRE.
Who from a bad man's boſom wards the blow
Reſerves the whetted dagger for his own.
Denounced twice—and twice I ſaved his life!

(Exit.)

BARRERE.
The ſections will ſupport then—there's the point!
No! he can never weather out the ſtorm—
Yet he is ſudden in revenge—No more!
I muſt away to Tallien.

(Exit.)

SCENE changes to the houſe of ADELAIDE.

ADELAIDE *enters, ſpeaking to a ſervant.*

ADELAIDE.
Didſt thou preſent the letter that I gave thee?

Did Tallien anfwer, he would foon return?

SERVANT.

He is in the Thuilleries—with him Legendre—
In deep difcourfe they feem'd: as I approach'd.
He waved his hand as bidding me retire:
I did not interrupt him.   (*Returns the letter.*)

ADELAIDE.

Thou didft rightly.
                    (*Exit. Servant.*)
O this new freedom! at how dear a price
We've bought the feeming good ! The peaceful virtues
And every blandifhment of private life,
The father's cares, the mother's fond endearment,
All facrificed to liberty's wild riot.
The winged hours, that fcatter'd rofes round me,
Languid and fad drag their flow courfe along,
And fhake big gall-drops from their heavy wings.
But I will fteal away thefe anxious thoughts
By the foft languifhment of warbled airs,
If haply melodies may lull the fenfe
Of forrow for a while.

S O F T   M U S I C.

Enter TALLIEN.

TALLIEN.

Mufic, my love? O breathe again that air !
Soft nurfe of pain, it fooths the weary foul
Of care, fweet as the whifper'd breeze of evening
That plays around the fick man's throbbing temples.

S O N G.

Tell me, on what holy ground
May domeftic peace be found ?

C

Halcyon daughter of the ſkies,
Far on fearful wing ſhe flies,
From the pomp of ſcepter'd ſtate,
From the rebel's noiſy hate.

In a cottag'd vale ſhe dwells
Liſt'ning to the Sabbath bells!
Still around her ſteps are ſeen,
Spotleſs honor's meeker mein,
Love, the fire of pleaſing fears,
Sorrow ſmiling through her tears,
And conſcious of the paſt employ,
Memory, boſom-ſpring of joy.

TALLIEN.

I thank thee, Adelaide! 'twas ſweet, though mournful.
But why thy brow o'ercaſt, thy cheek ſo wan?
Thou look'ſt as a lorn maid beſide ſome ſtream
That ſighs away the ſoul in fond deſpairing,
While ſorrow ſad, like the dank willow near her,
Hangs o'er the troubled fountain of her eye.

ADELAIDE.

Ah! rather let me aſk what myſtery lowers
On Tallien's darken'd brow. Thou doſt me wrong—
Thy ſoul diſtemper'd, can my heart be tranquil?

TALLIEN.

Tell me, by whom thy brother's blood was ſpilt?
Aſks he not vengeance on theſe patriot murderers?
It has been born too tamely. Fears and curſes
Groan on our midnight beds, and e'en our dreams
Threaten the aſſaſſin hand of Robeſpierre.
He dies!—nor has the plot eſcaped his fears.

ADELAIDE.

Yet—yet—be cautious! much I fear the Commune—

The tyrant's creatures, and their fate with his
Faſt link'd in cloſe indiſſoluble union.
The pale Convention—

TALLIEN.

       Hate him as they fear him,
Impatient of the chain, reſolv'd and ready.

ADELAIDE.

Th' enthuſiaſt mob, confuſion's lawleſs ſons—

TALLIEN.

They are aweary of his ſtern morality,
The fair-maſk'd offspring of ferocious pride.
The ſections too ſupport the delegates:
All—all is ours! e'en now the vital air
Of Liberty, condens'd awhile, is burſting
(Force irreſiſtable!) from its compreſſure—
To ſhatter the arch chemiſt in the exploſion!

Enter BILLAUD VARENNES *and* BOURDON L'OISE.

                (Adelaide retires.)

BOURDON L'OISE.

Tallien! was this a time for amorous conference?
Henriot, the tyrant's moſt devoted creature,
Marſhals the force of Paris; The fierce club,
With Vivier at their head, in loud acclaim
Have ſworn to make the guillotine in blood
Float on the ſcaffold.—But who comes here?

Enter BARRERE *abruptly.*

BARRERE.

Say, are ye friends to freedom? *I am her's!*
Let us, forgetful of all common feuds,
           C 2

Rally around her fhrine! E'en now the tyrant
Concerts a plan of inftant maffacre !

BILLAUD VARENNES.

Away to the Convention! with that voice
So oft the herald of glad victory,
Roufe their fallen fpirits, thunder in their ears
The name: of tyrant, plunderer, affaffin !
The violent workings of my foul within
Anticipate the monfter's blood !
      (Cry from the ftreet of—No Tyrant ! Down with
           the Tyrant !)

TALLIEN.

Hear ye that outcry ?—If the trembling members
Even for a moment hold his fate fufpended,
I fwear by the holy poniard, that ftabbed Cæfar,
This dagger probes his heart !
              (Exeunt omnes.)

ACT II.

SCENE, The Convention.

ROBESPIERRE *mounts the Tribune.*

Once more befits it that the voice of truth,
Fearlefs in innocence, though leagerd round
By envy and her hateful brood of hell,
Be heard amid this hall; once more befits
The patriot, whofe prophetic eye fo oft
Has pierced thro' faction's veil, to flafh on crimes
Of deadlieft import. Mouldering in the grave
Sleeps Capet's caitiff corfe ; my daring hand
Levelled to earth his blood-cemented throne,

My voice declared his guilt, and ftirred up France
To call for vengeance. I too dug the grave
Where fleep the Girondifts, detefted band !
Long with the fhew of freedom they abufed
Her ardent fons. Long time the well-turn'd phrafe
The high fraught fentence and the lofty tone
Of declamation thunder'd in this hall,
Till reafon midft a labyrinth of words
Perplex'd, in filence feem'd to yield affent.
I durft oppofe. Soul of my honoured friend,
Spirit of Marat upon thee I call—
Thou know'ft me faithful, know'ft with what warm zeal
I urg'd the caufe of juftice, ftripp'd the mafk
From factions deadly vifage, and deftroy'd
Her traitor brood. Whofe patriot arm hurl'd down
Hebert and Roufin, and the villain friends
Of Danton, foul apoftate ! thofe, who long
Mafk'd treafon's form in liberty's fair garb,
Long deluged France with blood, and durft defy
Omnipotence ! but I it feems am falfe !
I am a traitor too ! I—Robefpierre !
I—at whofe name the daftard defpot brood
Look pale with fear, and call on faints to help them !
Who dares accufe me ? who fhall dare belie
My fpotlefs name ? Speak, ye accomplice band,
Of what am I accus'd ? of what ftrange crime
Is Maximilian Robefpierre accus'd,
That through this hall the buz of difcontent
Should murmur ? who fhall fpeak ?

BILLAUD VARENNES.
                              O patriot tongue
Belying the foul heart ! Who was it urg'd
Friendly to tyrants that accurft decree,
Whofe influence brooding o'er this hallowed hall,
Has chill'd each tongue to filence. Who deftroyed
The freedom of debate, and carried through

The fatal law, that doom'd the delegates,
Unheard before their equals, to the bar
Where cruelty fat throned, and murder reign'd
With her Dumas coequal? Say—thou man
Of mighty eloquence, whofe law was that?

COUTHON.

That law was mine. I urged it—I propos'd—
The voice of France affembled in her fons
Affented, though the tame and timid voice
Of traitors murmur'd. I advis'd that law—
I juftify it. It was wife and good.

BARRERE.

Oh, wonderous wife and moft convenient too!
I have long mark'd thee, Robefpierre—and now
Proclaim thee traitor—tyrant!

(Loud applaufes.)

ROBESPIERRE.

It is well.

I am a traitor! oh, that I had fallen
When Regnault lifted high the murderous knife,
Regnault the inftrument belike of thofe
Who now themfelves would fain affaffinate,
And legalize their murders. I ftand here
An ifolated patriot—hemmed around
By factions noify pack; befet and bay'd
By the foul hell-hounds who know no efcape
From juftice' outftretch'd arm, but by the force
That pierces through her breaft.

(Murmurs, and fhouts of—Down with the tyrant!)

ROBESPIERRE.

Nay, but I will be heard. There was a time
When Robefpierre began, the loud applaufes
Of honeft patriots drown'd the honeft found.

But times are chang'd, and villainy prevails.

COLLOT D'HERBOIS.

No—villainy fhall fall. France could not brook
A monarch's fway—founds the dictator's name
More foothing to her ear ?

BOURDON L'OISE.

     Rattle her chains
More mufically now than when the hand
Of Briffot forged her fetters ; or the crew
Of Hebert thundered out their blafphemies,
And Danton talk'd of virtue ?

ROBESPIERRE.

     Oh, that Briffot
Were here again to thunder in this hall.
That Hebert lived, and Danton's giant form
Scowl'd once again defiance ! fo my foul
Might cope with worthy foes.
     People of France
Hear me ! Beneath the vengeance of the law,
Traitors have perifh'd countlefs; more furvive :
The hydra-headed faction lifts anew
Her daring front, and fruitful from her wounds,
Cautious from paft defects, contrives new wiles
Againft the fons of Freedom.

TALLIEN.

     Freedom lives !
Oppreffion falls—for France has felt her chains,
Has burft them too. Who traitor-like ftept forth
Amid the hall of Jacobines to fave
Camille Defmoulines, and the venal wretch
D'Eglantine ?

ROBESPIERRE.

I did—for I thought them honeſt.
And Heaven foreſend that vengeance ere ſhould ſtrike,
Ere juſtice doom'd the blow.

BARRERE.

Traitor, thou didſt.
Yes, the accomplice of their dark deſigns,
Awhile didſt thou defend them, when the ſtorm
Lower'd at ſafe diſtance. When the clouds frown'd darker,
Fear'd for yourſelf and left them to their fate.
Oh, I have mark'd thee long, and through the veil
Seen thy foul projects. Yes, ambitious man,
Self-will'd dictator o'er the realm of France,
The vengeance thou haſt plann'd for patriots,
Falls on thy head. Look how thy brother's deeds
Diſhonour thine ! He the firm patriot,
Thou the foul parricide of Liberty !

ROBESPIERRE, Junior.

Barrere—attempt not meanly to divide
Me from my brother. I partake his guilt,
For I partake his virtue.

ROBESPIERRE.

Brother, by my ſoul,
More dear I hold thee to my heart, that thus
With me thou dar'ſt to tread the dangerous path
Of virtue, than that nature twined her cords
Of kindred round us.

BARRERE.

Yes, allied in guilt,
Even as in blood ye are. Oh, thou worſt wretch,
Thou worſe than Sylla ! haſt thou not proſcrib'd
Yea, in moſt foul anticipation ſlaughter'd
Each patriot repreſentative of France ?

BOURDON L'OISE.

Was not the younger Cæfar too to reign
O'er all our valiant armies in the fouth,
And ftill continue there his merchant wiles?

ROBESPIERRE, Junior.

His merchant wiles! Oh, grant me patience, heaven!
Was it by merchant wiles I gain'd you back
Toulon, when proudly on her captive towers
Wav'd high the Englifh flag? or fought I then
With merchant wiles, when fword in hand I led
Your troops to conqueft? fought I merchant like,
Or barter'd I for victory, when death
Strode o'er the reeking ftreets with giant ftride,
And fhook his ebon plumes, and fternly fmil'd
Amid the bloody banquet? when appal'd
The hireling fons of England fpread the fail
Of fafety, fought I like a merchant then?
Oh, patience! patience!

BOURDON L'OISE.

                    How this younger tyrant
Mouths out defiance to us! even fo
He had led on the armies of the fouth,
Till once again the plains of France were drench'd
With her beft blood.

COLLOT D'HERBOIS.

                    Till once again difplay'd
Lyons' fad tragedy had call'd me forth
The minifter of wrath, whilft flaughter by
Had bathed in human blood.

DUBOIS CRANCE.

                    No wonder, friend,
That we are traitors—that our heads muft fall
Beneath the axe of death! when Cæfar-like
D

Reigns Robefpierre, 'tis wifely done to doom
The fall of Brutus.   Tell me, bloody man,
Haft thou not parcell'd out deluded France
As it had been fome province won in fight
Between your curft triumvirate.   You, Couthon,
Go with my brother to the fouthern plains ;
St. Juft, be yours the army of the north ;
Mean time I rule at Paris.

ROBESPIERRE.

                          Matchlefs knave !
What—not one blufh of confcience on thy cheek—
Not one poor blufh of truth ! moft likely tale !
That I who ruined Briffot's towering hopes,
I who difcovered Hebert's impious wiles,
And fharp'd for Danton's recreant neck the axe,
Should now be traitor ! had I been fo minded,
Think ye I had deftroyed the very men
Whofe plots refembled mine ? bring forth your proofs
Of this deep treafon.   Tell me in whofe breaft
Found ye the fatal fcroll ? or tell me rather
Who forg'd the fhamelefs falfhood ?

COLLOT D'HERBOIS.

                        Afk you proofs ?
Robefpierre, what proofs were afk'd when Briffot died ?

LEGENDRE.

What proofs adduced you when the Danton died ?
When at the imminent peril of my life
I rofe, and fearlefs of thy frowning brow,
Proclaim'd him guiltlefs ?

ROBESPIERRE.

                          I remember well
The fatal day.   I do repent me much
That I kill'd Cæfar and fpar'd Antony.

But I have been too lenient. I have ſpar'd
The ſtream of blood, and now my own muſt flow
To fill the current.

(Loud applauſes.)

Triumph not too ſoon,

Juſtice may yet be victor,

Enter St. Just, and mounts the Tribune.

St. Just.

I come from the committee—charged to ſpeak
Of matters of high import. I omit
Their orders. Repreſentatives of France,
Boldly in his own perſon ſpeaks St. Juſt
What his own heart ſhall dictate.

Tallien.

Hear ye this,

Inſulted delegates of France ? St. Juſt
From your committee comes—comes charg'd to ſpeak
Of matters of high import—yet omits
Their orders ! Repréſentatives of France,
That bold man I denounce, who diſobeys
The nations orders.—I denounce St. Juſt,

(Loud applauſes.)

St. Just,

Hear me!

(Violent murmurs.)

Robespierre.

He ſhall be heard !

Burdon l'Oise.

Muſt we contaminate this ſacred hall
With the foul breath of treaſon ?

D 2

Collot d'Herbois.

Drag him away!
Hence with him to the bar.

Couthon.

Oh, juſt proceedings!
Robeſpierre prevented liberty of ſpeech—
And Robeſpierre is a tyrant! Tallien reigns,
He dreads to hear the voice of innocence—
And St. Juſt muſt be ſilent!

Legendre.

Heed we well
That juſtice guide our actions. No light import
Attends this day. I move St. Juſt be heard.

Freron.

Inviolate be the ſacred right of man,
The freedom of debate.

(Violent applauſes.)

St. Juſt.

I may be heard then! much the times are chang'd,
When St. Juſt thanks this hall for hearing him.
Robeſpierre is call'd a tyrant. Men of France
Judge not too ſoon. By popular diſcontent
Was Ariſtides driven into exile,
Was Phocion murder'd? Ere ye dare pronounce
Robeſpierre is guilty, it befits ye well,
Conſider who accuſe him. Tallien,
Bourdon of Oiſe—the very men denounced,
For that their dark intrigues diſturb'd the plan
Of government. Legendre the ſworn friend
Of Danton fall'n apoſtate. Dubois Crance,
He who at Lyons ſpar'd the royaliſts—
Collot d'Herbois—

BOURDON L'OISE.
                    ·What—fhall the traitor rear
His head amid our tribune—and blafpheme
Each patriot? fhall the hireling flave of faction—

ST. JUST.
I am of no one faction.   I contend
Againft all factions.

TALLIEN.
                    I efpoufe the caufe
Of truth. Robefpierre on yefter morn pronounced
Upon his own authority a report.
To-day St. Juft comes down.   St. Juft neglects
What the committee orders, and harangues
From his own will.   O citizens of France
I weep for you—I weep for my poor country—
I tremble for the caufe of Liberty,
When individuals fhall affume the fway,
And with more infolence than kingly pride
Rule the republic.

BILLAUD VARENNES.
Shudder, ye reprefentatives of France,
Shudder with horror.   Henriot commands
The marfhall'd force of Paris.   Henriot,
Foul parricide—the fworn ally of Hebert
Denounced by all—upheld by Robefpierre.
Who fpar'd La Valette? who promoted him,
Stain'd with the deep die of nobility?
Who to an ex-peer gave the high command?
Who fcreen'd from juftice the rapacious thief?
Who caft in chains the friends of Liberty?
Robefpierre, the felf-ftil'd patriot Robefpierre—
Robefpierre, allied with villain Daubignè—
Robefpierre, the foul arch tyrant Robefpierre.

BOURDON, L'OISE.

He talks of virtue—of morality.—
Confiftent patriot ! he Daubigne's friend !!
Henriot's fupporter virtuous ! preach of virtue,
Yet league with villains, for with Robefpierre
Villains alone ally.   Thou art a tyrant !
I ftile thee tyrant Robefpierre !

(Loud applaufes.)

ROBESPIERRE.

Take back the name.   Ye citizens of France—

(Violent clamour.   Cries of—Down with the Tyrant!)

TALLIEN.

Oppreffion falls.   The traitor ftands appall'd—
Guilt's iron fangs engrafp his fhrinking foul—
He hears affembled France denounce his crimes !
He fees the mafk torn from his fecret fins——
He trembles on the precipice of fate.
Fall'n guilty tyrant ! murder'd by thy rage
How many an innocent victim's blood has ftain'd
Fair freedom's altar ! Sylla-like thy hand
Mark'd down the virtues, that, thy foes removed,
Perpetual Dictator thou might'ft reign,
And tyrannize o'er France, and call it freedom !
Long time in timid guilt the traitor plann'd
His fearful wiles—fuccefs emboldened fin—
And his ftretch'd arm had grafp'd the diadem
Ere now, but that the coward's heart recoil'd,
Left France awak'd, fhould roufe her from her dream,
And call aloud for vengeance.   He, like Cæfar,
With rapid ftep urged on his bold career,
Even to the fummit of ambitious power,
And deem'd the name of King alone was wanting.
Was it for this we hurl'd proud Capet down ?
Is it for this we wage eternal war
Againft the tyrant horde of murderers,

The crowned cockatrices whofe foul venom
Infects all Europe? was it then for this
We fwore to guard our liberty with life,
That Robefpierre fhould reign? the fpirit of freedom
Is not yet funk fo low. The glowing flame
That animates each honeft Frenchman's heart
Not yet extinguifh'd. I invoke thy fhade,
Immortal Brutus! I too wear a dagger;
And if the reprefentatives of France,
Through fear or favor fhould delay the fword
Of juftice, Tallien emulates thy virtues;
Tallien, like Brutus, lifts the avenging arm;
Tallien fhall fave his country.

(Violent applaufes.)

BILLAUD VARENNES.
                                  I demand
The arreft of all the traitors. Memorable
Will be this day for France.

ROBESPIERRE.
                             Yes! Memorable
This day will be for France——for villains triumph.

LEBAS.
I will not fhare in this day's damning guilt.
Condemn me too.

(Great cry—Down with the Tyrants!)

(The two Robefpierres, Couthon, St. Juft, and Lebas
are led off.)

A C T III.

SCENE Continues.

COLLOT D'HERBOIS.

Cæsar is fallen ! The baneful tree of Java,
Whose death-diſtilling boughs dropt poiſonous dew,
Is rooted from its baſe. This worſe than Cromwell,
The auſtere, the ſelf denying Robeſpierre,
Even in this hall, where once with terror mute
We liſtened to the hypocrite's harangues,
Has heard his doom.

BILLAUD VARENNES.

        Yet muſt we not ſuppoſe
The tyrant will fall tamely. His ſworn hireling
Henriot, the daring deſperate Henriot
Commands the force of Paris. I denounce him.

FRERON.

l denounce Fluriot too, the mayor of Paris.

Enter DUBOIS CRANCE.

DUBOIS CRANCE.

Robeſpierre is reſcued. Henriot at the head
Of the arm'd force has reſcued the fierce tyrant.

COLLOT D'HERBOIS.

Ring the tocſin—call all the citizens
To ſave their country—never yet has Paris
Forſook the repreſentatives of France.

TALLIEN.

It is the hour of danger.   I propofe
This fitting be made permanent.

(Loud applaufes.)

COLLOT D'HERBOIS.

The national Convention fhall remain
Firm at its poft.

Enter a MESSENGER.

MESSENGER.

Robefpierre has reach'd the Commune.   They efpoufe
The tyrant's caufe.   St. Juft is up in arms!
St. Juft—the young ambitious bold St. Juft
Harangues the mob.   The fanguinary Couthon
Thirfts for your blood.

(Tocfin rings.)

TALLIEN.

Thefe tyrants are in arms againft the law:
Outlaw the rebels.

Enter MERLIN OF DOUAY.

MERLIN.

Health to the reprefentatives of France!
I paft this moment through the armed force—
They afk'd my name—and when they heard a delegate,
Swore I was not the friend of France.

COLLOT D'HERBOIS.

The tyrants threaten us as when they turn'd
The cannon's mouth on Briffot.

E

Enter another MESSENGER.

SECOND MESSENGER.

Vivier harangues the Jacobins—the club
Efpoufe the caufe of Robefpierre.

Enter another MESSENGER.

THIRD MESSENGER.

All's loft—the tyrant triumphs.   Henriot leads
The foldiers to his aid.——Already I hear
The rattling cannon deftin'd to furround
This facred hall.

TALLIEN.

Why, we will die like men then.
The reprefentatives of France dare death,
When duty fteels their bofoms.

(Loud applaufes.)

TALLIEN *addreffing the galleries.*

Citizens !

France is infulted in her delegates—
The majefty of the republic is infulted—
Tyrants are up in arms.   An armed force
Threats the Convention.   The Convention fwears
To die, or fave the country !

(Violent applaufes from the galleries.)

CITIZEN *from above.*

We too fwear
To die, or fave the country.   Follow me.

(All the men quit the galleries.)

Enter another MESSENGER.

FOURTH MESSENGER.
Henriot is taken !—

(Loud applauses.)

Henriot is taken.   Three of your brave foldiers
Swore they would feize the rebel flave of tyrants,
Or perifh in the attempt.   As he patroll'd
The ftreets of Paris, ftirring up the mob,
They feiz'd him.

(Applauses.)

BILLAUD VARENNES.
   Let the names of thefe brave men
Live to the future day.

Enter BOURDON L'OISE *fword in hand.*

BOURDON L'OISE.
I have clear'd the Commune.

(Applauses.)

     Through the throng I rufh'd,
Brandifhing my good fword to drench its blade
Deep in the tyrant's heart.   The timid rebels
Gave way.   I met the foldiery—I fpake
Of the dictator's crimes—of patriots chain'd
In dark deep dungeons by his lawlefs rage—
Of knaves fecure beneath his foftering power,
I fpake of Liberty.   Their honeft hearts
Caught the warm flame,   The general fhout burft forth,
" Live the Convention—Down with Robefpierre !"

(Applauses.)

(Shouts from without—Down with the tyrant!)

TALLIEN.
I hear, I hear the foul-infpiring founds,
France fhall be faved ! her generous fons attached.

E 2

To principles, not perfons, fpurn the idol
They worfhipp'd once. Yes, Robefpierre fhall fall
As Capet fell! Oh! never let us deem
That France fhall crouch beneath a tyrant's throne,
That the almighty people who have broke
On their oppreffors heads the oppreffive chain,
Will court again their fetters! eafier were it
To hurl the cloud-capt mountain from its bafe,
Than force the bonds of flavery upon men
Determined to be free!

(Applaufes.)

Enter LEGENDRE—*A piftol in one hand. Keys in the other.*

LEGENDRE. *Flinging down the keys.*
So—let the mutinous Jacobins meet now
In the open air.

(Loud applaufes.)

    A factious turbulent party
Lording it o'er the ftate fince Danton died,
And with him the Cordeliers.—A hireling band
Of loud-tongued orators controull'd the club,
And bade them bow the knee to Robefpierre.
Vivier has 'fcap'd me. Curfe his coward heart—
This fate-fraught tube of Juftice in my hand
I rufh'd into the hall. He mark'd mine eye
That beam'd its patriot anger, and flafh'd full
With death-denouncing meaning. 'Mid the throng
He mingled. I purfued—but ftaid my hand,
Left haply I might fhed the innocent blood.

(Applaufes.)

FRERON.
They took from me my ticket of admiffion—
Expell'd me from their fittings.—Now, forfooth,
Humbled and trembling re-infert my name.

But Freron enters not the club again
'Till it be purg'd of guilt—'till, purified
Of tyrants and of traitors, honeſt men
May breathe the air in ſafety.

(Shouts from without.)

BARRERE.

What means this uproar ! if the tyrant band
Should gain the people once again to riſe—
We are as dead !

TALLIEN.

And wherefore fear we death ?
Did Brutus fear it ? or the Grecian friends
Who buried in Hipparchus breaſt the ſword,
And died triumphant ? Cæſar ſhould fear death,
Brutus muſt ſcorn the bugbear.

*(Shouts from without. Live the Convention—Down
with the Tyrants!)*

TALLIEN.

Hark ! again
The ſounds of honeſt Freedom !

Enter DEPUTIES *from the* SECTIONS.

CITIZEN.

Citizens ! repreſentatives of France !
Hold on your ſteady courſe. The men of Paris
Eſpouſe your cauſe. The men of Paris ſwear
They will defend the delegates of Freedom.

TALLIEN.

Hear ye this, Colleagues ? hear ye this, my brethren ?
And does no thrill of joy pervade your breaſts ?
My boſom bounds to rapture. I have ſeen

The fons of France fhake off the tyrant yoke;
I have, as much as lies in mine own arm,
Hurl'd down the ufurper.—Come death when it will
I have lived long enough.

(Shouts without.)

BARRERE.

Hark! how the noife increafes! through the gloom
Of the ftill evening—harbinger of death
Rings the tocfin! the dreadful generale
Thunders through Paris—

(Cry without—Down with the Tyrant!)

Enter LECOINTRE.

LECOINTRE.

So may eternal juftice blaft the foes
Of France! fo perifh all the tyrant brood,
As Robefpierre has perifhed! Citizens,
Cæfar is taken.

(Loud and repeated applaufes.)

I marvel not, that with fuch fearlefs front,
He braved our vengeance, and with angry eye
Scowled round the hall defiance. He relied
On Henriot's aid—the Commune's villain friendfhip,
And Henriot's *boughten* fuccours. Ye have heard
How Henriot refcued him—how with open arms
The Commune welcom'd in the rebel tyrant—
How Fluriot aided, and feditious Vivier
Stirr'd up the Jacobins. All had been loft—
The reprefentatives of France had perifh'd—
Freedom had funk beneath the tyrant arm
Of this foul parricide, but that her fpirit
Infpir'd the men of Paris. Henriot call'd
" To arms" in vain, whilft Bourdon's patriot voice
Breath'd eloquence, and o'er the Jacobins

Legendre frown'd difmay. The tyrants fled—
They reach'd the Hotel. We gather'd round—we call'd
For vengeance! Long time, obftinate in defpair
With knives they hack'd around them. 'Till foreboding
The fentence of the law, the clamorous cry
Of joyful thoufands hailing their deftruction,
Each fought by fuicide to efcape the dread
Of death. Lebas fucceeded. From the window
Leapt the younger Robefpierre, but his fractur'd limb
Forbade to efcape. The felf-will'd dictator
Plung'd often the keen knife in his dark breaft,
Yet impotent to die. He lives all mangled
By his own tremulous hand! All gafh'd and gored
He lives to tafte the bitternefs of death.
Even now they meet their doom. The bloody Couthon,
The fierce St. Juft, even now attend their tyrant
To fall beneath the axe. I faw the torches
Flafh on their vifages a dreadful light—
I faw them whilft the black blood roll'd adown
Each ftern face, even then with dauntlefs eye
Scowl round contemptuous, dying as they lived,
Fearlefs of fate !

(Loud and repeated applaufes.)

Barrere mounts the Tribune.

For ever hallowed be this glorious day,
When Freedom, burfting her oppreffive chain,
Tramples on the oppreffor. When the tyrant
Hurl'd from his blood-cemented throne, by the arm
Of the almighty people, meets the death
He plann'd for thoufands. Oh ! my fickening heart
Has funk within me, when the various woes
Of my brave country crowded o'er my brain
In ghaftly numbers—when affembled hordes

Dragg'd from their hovels by defpotic power
Rufh'd o'er her frontiers, plunder'd her fair hamlets,
And fack'd her populous towns, and drench'd with
    blood
The reeking fields of Flanders.—When within,
Upon her vitals prey'd the rankling tooth
Of treafon ; and oppreffion, giant form,
Trampling on freedom, left the alternative
Of flavery, or of death. Even from that day,
When, on the guilty Capet, I pronounced
The doom of injured France, has faction reared
Her hated head amongft us. Roland preach'd
Of mercy—the uxorious dotard Roland,
The woman-govern'd Roland durft afpire
To govern France ; and Petion talk'd of virtue,
And Vergniaud's eloquence, like the honeyed tongue
Of fome foft Syren wooed us to deftruction.
We triumphed over thefe. On the fame fcaffold
Where the laft Louis pour'd his guilty blood,
Fell Briffot's head, the womb of darkfome treafons,
And Orleans, villain kinfman of the Capet,
And Hebert's atheift crew, whofe maddening hand
Hurl'd down the altars of the living God,
With all the infidels intolerance.
The laft worft traitor triumphed—triumph'd long,
Secur'd by matchlefs villainy. By turns
Defending and deferting each accomplice
As intereft prompted. In the goodly foil
Of Freedom, the foul tree of treafon ftruck
Its deep-fix'd roots, and dropt the dews of death
On all who flumbered in its fpecious fhade.
He wove the web of treachery. He caught
The liftening crowd by his wild eloquence,
His cool ferocity that perfuaded murder,
Even whilft it fpake of mercy !—never, never
Shall this regenerated country wear

The defpot yoke.   Though myriads round affail,
And with worfe fury urge this new crufade
Than favages have known ; though the leagued defpots
Depopulate all Europe, fo to pour
The accumulated mafs upon our coafts,
Sublime amid the florm fhall France arife,
And like the rock amid furrounding waves
Repel the rufhing ocean.—She fhall wield
The thunder-bolt of vegeance—fhe fhall blaft
The defpot's pride, and liberate the world !

F I N I S.